BUTTON
and His Surprising Capers

BUTTON
and His Surprising Capers

John D. Drenchko

VANTAGE PRESS
New York

FIRST EDITION

All rights reserved, including the right of
reproduction in whole or in part in any form.

Copyright © 1992 by John D. Drenchko

Published by Vantage Press, Inc.
516 West 34th Street, New York, New York 10001

Manufactured in the United States of America
ISBN: 0-533-10021-6

Library of Congress Catalog Card No.: 91-91107

0 9 8 7 6 5 4 3 2 1

To my sister Ethell,
who took such good care of Button
during my stay in the hospital

Preface

It has been approximately three years since *A True Story about Button* was written and published. It was a story about the first two years of Button's life.

To acquaint the reader with why the first book was written, a short narration I believe is in order.

From the very first week that Button was acquired from a pet shop, I noticed a certain alertness and intelligence about him not usually attributed to rabbits. Even at the pet store, of all the bunnies there he seemed to stand out—sitting up and unafraid when I poked a finger through the wire mesh of the cage to touch and stroke him.

The cute lop ears and the color of his fur, which is basically white with an even dispersion of brown on the head, back, and sides, also tended to further attract me to him.

As weeks went by there was always some new surprise from Button, with his capabilities and antics. Therefore I felt I just had to write a story about him. Rather than risk forgetting some interesting incident, I began to keep notes on his actions. That is how *A True Story about Button* came about.

As time went on, week after week, after his second birthday, I continued taking notes, for Button never ceased to amaze my sister and myself. He was truly a member of the family, as any pet can be. I therefore decided to write a sequel to *A True Story about Button*—all true accounts of the following three years of his life.

Of course Button was trained regarding his "bathroom needs." Since he wasn't partial to a cat litter box, as he scattered the contents in all directions, newspapers were placed in a corner of the basement for his use. After periodically placing him on the papers from time to time, my sister Terry or I would stand by. It did not take Button long to learn what was expected of him. Thereafter he used the corner when the need arose, even if he was upstairs in the kitchen or living room. We always made sure the basement door was at least partially open for him to go there.

Button learned to go up and down stairs with ease—which is unusual for a rabbit. I had other pet bunnies even as a youngster, but none learned to go up or down stairs.

This brings to mind a conversation I had with a young lady recently who read *A True Story about Button*. She said when she and her sister were young girls the sister had a pet white rabbit. That bunny got out of its box one night in the kitchen, climbed the stairs to the second floor, found their bedroom, and leaped upon the bed of one of the girls asleep in bed and nuzzled up close to her face until she awakened. This certainly indicates what a keen sense of smell a bunny has and how intelligent some can be. If a person plays with and cuddles a small animal frequently, it will be able to follow the lingering body scent of that person even in the dark.

Today as I went to the basement door leading to the breezeway to put out some birdseed for the birds, Button quickly followed. I had a piece of folded newspaper in a crack between the door and frame at the bottom, which I hadn't yet gotten around to repairing, to keep the cold air out. However, the first thing Button did before I opened the door was get ahold of the paper with his teeth, pull it out, and toss it aside. That was his job every morning.

By the time I picked up the bird food, Button was already waiting at the breezeway door leading to the outside. He loves going out for a few minutes even if it is cold. I was undecided as to whether I should let him out with me, as it was late February and about twenty-eight degrees Fahrenheit out there with snow on the ground. Being an indoor bunny, Button is not acclimated to that kind of temperature. However, since I was only going to be out for a few minutes, I decided to let him out with me.

I placed the birdseed in the feeding boxes and some on the driveway where the snow was partially cleared, as the doves seemed to prefer eating there. I noticed Button had hopped along the cleared walk alongside the house and up a few steps to the veranda and was waiting by the door leading to the kitchen to be let into the house that way. I concluded the temperature was just not to his liking. However, as I was headed back to the breezeway door I called to Button and he lost no time in scampering back with me the way he came. I'm sure what was going through his mind—and if he could talk, he would say, "I'll wait for warmer weather."

This, however, brings to mind a day in December when we had our first light snowfall. (This incident I forgot to jot down among my notes.) As the snow was rather wet, it piled up in small clusters as the walks were cleared.

Usually on a day like that I let Button come up only into the breezeway and workshop area while I got the feed for our feathered friends. However, since it wasn't too cold I let Button out while I attended to feeding the birds.

As I was headed back toward the breezeway door, I noticed Button at a small mound of snow that seemed to intrigue him. Knowing his curiosity, I therefore stopped to watch for a few moments. It did not surprise me when he began sampling some of it. I guess it was too cold for his tongue, for he stopped eating it and went at the small pile of snow with his front paws with gusto, probably thinking how easy this "white stuff" was to dig into. This went on for two or three minutes. Button then stopped and began shaking his paws. I guess the cold snow was too much for him and not as much fun as he thought at first. I then guided him back toward the door and the basement. I am sure he welcomed the warmth of the indoors again as he hopped over to his dishes of food.

However, the days went by quite quickly—so it seemed—and soon it was well into spring, with flowers blooming and grass ready for frequent mowings. Also, nice days to do outdoor work. I am sure that Button enjoyed the weather, as he wasn't so anxious to come in too soon.

Today I decided to repair an outdoor bench. As it was quite nice out, I decided to bring Button out, too. He never misses an opportunity to "assist" me—checking out the tools in the tool caddy or the necessary materials. If it's something in a bag, he soon gets to it, working it over with his front paws trying to tear it apart. After a while he tires of that and looks for something else of interest to do, such as going into the garage or the adjacent workshop. Since I am close by I can keep an eye on him.

It was necessary to remove and replace a board

Button attempts to walk up to the bench, but the board is too steep and he slides back to the ground.

from the bench. After doing so I placed it so one end leaned on the bench and the other end on the concrete driveway. I then began taking some measurements. Although I noticed Button was now back and near the board, I did not pay attention as to what he was up to at the moment, as I was just concluding the final measurement.

It was then I noticed Button attempting to walk up upon the six-inch-wide board from the driveway to the seat of the bench. I just watched, as the incline of the board was at quite a high angle.

When he got about three-quarters of the way up, down he came sliding backward to the pavement. I just laughed and wondered what he would do if I reduced the incline to a smaller angle. This I did and sat back to watch. Knowing Button was a determined bunny from past antics, I wasn't surprised to see him make another attempt to get to the bench. This time he made it to the top with ease. Now normally Button would leap up upon the bench with little effort, but knowing his determination to try something different, I was not surprised by his trying something other than his usual method.

Whenever I was involved in some project and I knew Button would be around I kept a camera handy, for I never knew when one of his capers would present an interesting picture.

One night as I was getting ready for bed, I went about the usual chore of getting Button set for the night, which included preparing a small snack for him. This consisted of some wheat bread and rolled oats. He likes the ends of the bread, which is broken up into small pieces. Button looks forward to this preparation and watches my every move as I go about getting it ready. When I finish and head for the basement door he is right behind me. Needless to say, no second invitation is necessary as I place the dishes down alongside those containing pellets and water. I then change his water, make sure his night-light is on, and head upstairs. Button seems to know it is time to retire. After he finishes eating, he then stretches out under the table on a carpet or on a rug at the foot of the stairs. The basement door in the kitchen is left open in case he wishes to come back up and sleep in the kitchen or vestibule. Since part of the basement is finished as living quarters, Button likes to spend most of the night there, favoring two or three places where he sleeps.

Before retiring to my room, I usually check a number of items, such as adjusting the open casement window or thermostat setting in the living room. As I walked by the open basement door back to the kitchen, I glanced down the stairs and noticed Button already napping at the bottom. I left the screen barrier separating the kitchen and living room–hallway area open while I checked the locked outside door, then pulled up the weights of the cuckoo clock and turned out the light.

I went into my bedroom after closing the screen. (I do this because my sister usually retires before I do.) As a rule I undressed in the semidarkness, as there was sufficient light coming in the window from a nearby street lamp.

After taking my shirt off, and as I was about to place it on an easy chair in a corner, I noticed something white on the chair that I assumed to be a piece of apparel and was about to let the shirt drop on top of it. Was I startled when the "white item" moved! Of course, what else but Button? During that short period of time while I was doing the usual chores in the kitchen, he came up the stairs and promptly into my bedroom and settled down in the easy chair. I was reluctant in taking him back into the kitchen—but it was necessary in order for both of us to get some rest.

Today I decided to do some writing sitting on a footstool at the entrance of the two-car garage. It is early summer but cool and comfortable after an earlier rain. Button is alongside me taking a nap. But only after I settled down to write did he come over to me and stand up with his front paws on my leg. That was a request to scratch his nose, ears, and back. Button loves that, as most animals do. After accommodating him for a few minutes and to his satisfaction, I then continued to write. However, before I sat down to write I had earlier placed a two-foot-high foldable screen barrier across the entire entrance of the garage. It takes but a minute to put up or take down. This I found necessary to keep Button from wandering to the grass, where he would soon pick up fleas during the summer months. The grass becomes infested usually in June with these insects, and it lasts until the first good frost.

Since Button could not tell me what kind of screen he would prefer, I tried placing myself in his position. I know his preference would be no screen at all. I would liked to have used a wire with large holes that he could look through without the interwoven sections interfering with his view, yet holes small enough so he could not squeeze through. However, I recalled reading an article on rabbit teeth written by a veterinarian who writes for a rabbit magazine to which I subscribe. He mentioned that rabbits have a tendency to sometimes break their front teeth when they get hold of wire. Therefore, if a tooth is broken, it will not meet the

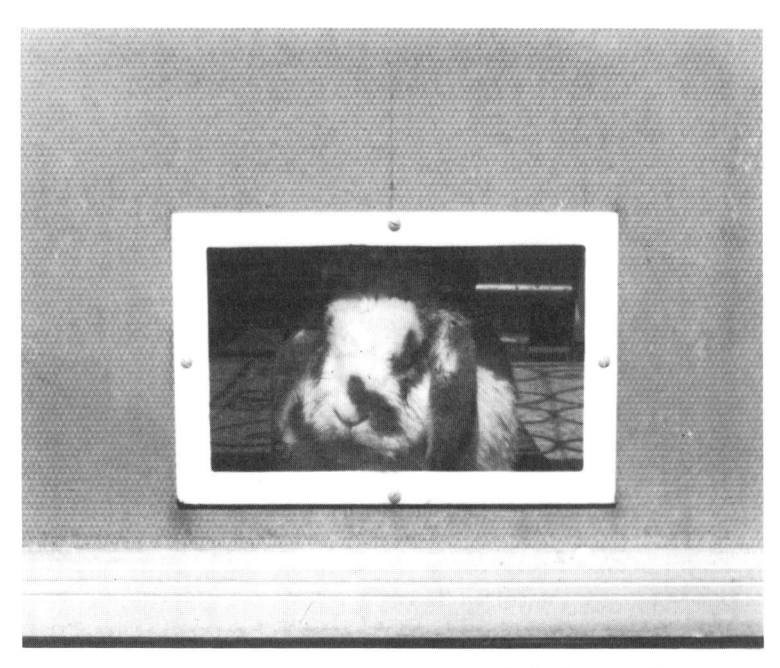

"I would rather be outside looking in."

opposite tooth for even wear, causing the unbroken tooth to grow inward, which becomes a problem for the rabbit. I therefore used chicken wire with small holes so Button could not reach through and get a grip with his teeth. Also, one panel of the barrier had a regular window screen, in case he preferred looking through that. However, I put myself in Button's place and looking through the wires found the view somewhat obstructed. Perhaps later I can come up with something better.

While on the subject of teeth, I recall when Button was still quite young he began chewing on the telephone cords and TV lead-in lines. It was necessary to put them out of his reach by running the wires through hard plastic tubing. At one time he chewed the telephone extension line in the living room so badly before it was discovered that it was necessary to replace it. I called the telephone company for a new one. A girl answered, and when I told her what happened she really had a good laugh. She probably heard that one for the first time.

A rabbit as a rule has twenty-eight teeth, those to chew with and the front or incisor teeth, two upper and two lower, used to bite off bits of food. These front ones can be a problem, as they never stop growing. However, to prevent them from getting too long, the cottontails usually gnaw on something hard, such as wood. Wild bunnies will chew on fallen tree branches or small growing trees, while the domestic ones will gnaw at the wooden part of their cages if the owners fail to provide them with something suitable to chew upon. Usually pet stores carry small hard wooden blocks of different shapes that one can buy for small animals to gnaw on to help keep their incisor teeth at the proper length.

As Button grew older he did very little chewing upon hard objects, even if he was given some choice cuttings from fruit trees, such as apple or plum. I noticed his front teeth began to get too long, with a tendency to curve inward to the roof of the mouth. It was therefore necessary to have them clipped to the proper level, as it was beginning to interfere with his eating.

I took Button to a veterinarian, and while I held my bunny the doctor quickly clipped the incisors with special clippers. I wasn't sure just how to hold Button, so the doctor showed me the proper grip. I took Button a second time in about two months to have his teeth clipped again.

However, when I learned the incisors never stop growing and Button needed to have it done again, I would attempt to do it at home. For a person to do it alone would be quite difficult. It really was a two-person undertaking. I therefore asked my friend and neighbor to assist me. I showed Jim just how to hold Button, with the two ears and the loose skin at the nape of the neck in one hand and the other one on the back or underneath the body. This prevented Button from moving his head. I then opened his mouth with one hand and quickly clipped the teeth with special clippers with the other, taking care that I did not cut his gums. Of course the hands were thoroughly washed and the clippers sterilized. The whole operation takes one to two minutes. I am sure Button did not care very much for this procedure but felt much better when eating afterward.

Unfortunately, it was necessary to repeat the above process about every ten to twelve weeks, but Jim was always very obliging and ready to assist me. I am sure Button would prefer to have this done in familiar surroundings rather than at the animal clinic.

I recall when my sister or I took our dog, Penny, to the veterinarian, while we were holding her waiting in the reception room she would get quite fidgety, jump to the floor, and head for the door. She knew from past visits the place was synonymous with pain. I heard a number of people relating the same experience with their pet cats and dogs.

Button has been trying to make friends with the three wild bunnies that live under the large evergreen trees in our yard for some time now. He still cannot get close to them. However, I manage to approach them within about three or four feet. I speak to them when I see them close by, and they will just sit there looking up at me. I make sure they have water and some cracked corn near the garden and evergreen trees. Occasionally I'll put out an apple or two and some rabbit pellets. They love the fruit but do not care too much for the domestic bunny food. In fact, they have become so used to me that when they see me carrying the water and feed they come hopping close to where I usually put it down near the trees. Seldom are all three cottontails together. Sometimes two of them come and other times there is only one.

Button is somewhat larger than the wild bunnies; perhaps that is why they back off when he approaches them. Of course one would think my size would scare them off—so perhaps it's something in the nature of trusting other animals only to a certain extent. Then again it may be the way I talk to them, trying to keep my voice down and even, or perhaps it is because I give them food and water. I also have a name for them. Since it is difficult to tell one from the other as they all have similar white markings, I use the same name for all three.

During the winter months I put the food out under an evergreen tree, as it is a shelter and seldom will snow penetrate through the thick needles. I have given them alfalfa pellets, the same that Button eats, as they are specially formulated with vitamins and minerals. Button loves them, but not so with his "cousins." Several times I tried some nice, juicy carrots. Although carrots are beloved by rabbits in stories, comics, and cartoons, neither Button nor the wild bunnies much cared for them.

This brings to mind a time in the fall when it occurred to me I had not seen the wild bunnies for about a week. One can usually see them just about every day. I asked a neighbor who always puts out apples under a tree for them. He remarked that he hadn't seen them for at least two weeks and noticed the apples had not been touched. Bill and I were fearful a stray dog or cat may have gotten hold of them. There are two or three large cats not belonging to anyone that prowl around the neighborhood.

Although these rabbits are alert and fast, I thought they might have been caught off guard.

I put corn out in the back adjacent to the garden as I previously mentioned, and as it was gone by evening, I assumed the bunnies ate it. Since the apples were not eaten in Bill's yard, I came to the conclusion that the birds found and ate the corn. I therefore was surprised and elated when I spotted one of the rabbits in the back by the feeding place. He appeared to be the larger and older of the trio. Soon as I called to him, he quickly hopped toward me. I believe he was glad to see me, too. I promptly went to the workshop and obtained some corn. When I got back he was still nearby and waiting. When I put the corn down, he went at it as if he had really missed that food.

Bill happened to be nearby in his yard, so I called to him and pointed to our "friend" eating away. He was as delighted as I was that one of them was back, as they are a pleasure to have about. However, we keep looking for the other two and are hopeful they will show up, too.

When God made this Earth, with plants, flowers, grass, trees, and all that is beautiful, he also knew human beings needed more than each other. What a dull world this would be without his mammals and birds. How much pleasure and companionship they bring to young and older people alike.

One day a young neighbor from across the street

came over to visit while I was sitting outside on a bench reading a newspaper. Button was just inside his fence at the entrance to the garage—stretched out and enjoying a nap.

As John was walking down the driveway, he had one arm behind his back. I thought this was kind of odd. When he got to where I was sitting he brought his arm to the front of him, holding a cute young kitten in his hand. He wanted to know if I wanted to adopt tabby as a playmate for Button. I was certainly tempted. I am sure he would have played with the kitten. But I had to think ahead, knowing that as it grew to maturity, it would have a tendency to go wandering. Two main reasons I had to decline John's offer were uppermost in my mind: the possibility of it being hit by a car and also the fact that the birds would stay away as, of course, a cat is a natural enemy of the small feathered creatures. As it was, we loved to see them feeding at their usual place every day. I am sure Button also enjoys watching them hopping about just a few feet from his wire barrier and not minding him at all.

John said he found the kitten wandering around on a side road quite a distance from the nearest house. Since he also loves animals, he had picked it up and put it in the car. When he got home the first thing he did was feed the little stray. The kitten could not seem to eat enough, attesting to the fact it had not had food for quite a while.

However, that evening after he brought it over to see if I wanted to adopt it John found a home for the little foundling. A friend of the family upon seeing the kitten promptly fell in love with it and took it home.

I usually get up around 7:30 A.M. or a little earlier and my sister a few minutes before that. But sometimes before either of us gets up, Button is heard in the kitchen. Sometimes he will get a little impatient and bang on the screen at the entrance to the living room and hallway to hurry us to be up and about.

As the screen is moved, Button loses no time hopping into the living room and then hallway. He is so elated he proceeds, setting speed records to my room then down to my sister Terry's room or the spare room and back again. One can understand a pet such as a dog or even a puppy scampering about in delight. But to see a bunny do that just makes one laugh at the antics.

Of course the first thing I do is the usual routine of putting out food for the birds. There is no point in taking care of Button with his food, as he would only stop eating to go outside with me. That is a priority with him.

If Button could speak and was asked what his favorite food is, I am sure he would say, "Banana." When we come back into the basement, he promptly heads for the foot of the stairs. There he waits until I am ready to go up to the kitchen. But if I pause to do something first, he becomes impatient and goes halfway up the stairs and keeps looking back at me, as if to say, "How long are you going to putter around?" Sensing his impatience, I decide to go on up, for I know what is on Button's mind—banana. Soon as I start up the steps, up he goes and awaits at the dish for that delicious food, which he promptly gets. Sometimes Terry already has it waiting for him. Even though bananas are almost a complete food, Button gets only a small piece, which is usually to his satisfaction. After that he partakes of some bread and oat flakes and then stretches out and relaxes under the table.

It is now well into spring again and quite warm outside. On one of these mornings we went through the same procedure in feeding the birds, with Button leading the way. Sometimes he is in quite a happy mood and delighted when we go out. It is such a pleasure to see him leap into the air and prance about, much like a frisky colt.

There doesn't seem to be a single bird in sight, and yet as the door of the breezeway is closed behind us, in a few moments the feeding area is swarming with a variety of our feathered friends. They must have "scouts" placed in strategic places to give the signal—"it's mealtime."

I have often marveled how intelligent mammals and birds can be. I am sure almost everyone has witnessed some act of unusual brainpower used by a pet or the undomesticated variety.

One normally would not associate unusual intelligence with rabbits. But if given a chance and especially if there is close relationship with a pet bunny, one could really be surprised. I have had a number of people relate to me how their pet rabbit surprised them with some novel antic. It is not just instinct but pure thinking on the bunny's part. I have witnessed this so many times with Button.

As also happened this one morning—it occurred to me I forgot to bring in the box containing the bird feed. I disliked disturbing the feeding birds, but I know as soon as I left again, they would promptly be back to continue eating.

Of course Button darted out with me, and while I retrieved the box he quickly hopped up to and on the veranda and up to the door leading to the kitchen. I

"How is this pose?"

followed him saying, "Okay, if that's the way you want to go into the house, I'll let you in." I opened the door and he promptly entered. I then closed the door and headed for the workshop to put the bird feed back. Perhaps Button figured I would follow him into the kitchen. However, I decided to quickly pick up a few strands of clover in the back part of the yard—so I went out through another door in the breezeway leading there. I left it opened, since I figured Button was in the house—so I thought. I picked a handful of his favorite greens, and as I turned around, there he was making a fast beeline toward me. I must have left the basement door ajar. Of course I was surprised. I expected him to linger in the kitchen, where Terry usually talks to him and gives him a stroke or two on the back as she goes about her work preparing breakfast. Or I thought if he went directly to the basement, he would spend a little time looking for me first. But as he saw the door open there, he lost no time getting to the top of the landing. And when Button saw the breezeway door opened, he had it all figured out, and he was right. I just laughed in amazement and showed him the clover, and he promptly followed me back to the breezeway and basement, where I gave him the greens. Of course he went at them with zest. I believe that in some ways animals outthink human beings.

Button has an insatiable curiosity. He needs to check out everything new to him and, of course, accessible. One day I was ready to do some typing in the living room. I set the portable typewriter on a small table, drew up a chair, and left the room to obtain some last writing accessory. Somewhat earlier I had noticed Button was taking a nap under the table in the kitchen. When I got back, however, there he was on my chair with his front paws on the typewriter keyboard and in no hurry to leave. Since my camera was on the credenza, it took me but a few moments to take his picture in that position.

Even after I took a couple of poses of him, he was in no hurry to relinquish my place at the typewriter. There was something about it that appealed to Button, for every time I set the typewriter up if he was around he jumped up on the chair, putting his paws on the keyboard.

One day I was sitting at a small table in the basement. Upon it was an early-model computer, with a separate keyboard and tape recorder alongside. It had been some time since I had used it, and I had decided to play around with the equipment for a while. The table was located in a corner with a bench along one side. On this bench was a small trunk and neatly stacked on top a variety of spare carpets and throw rugs. I guessed Button was either upstairs in the kitchen or taking a nap on an easy chair on the other side of the basement out of my view because of drapes separating a section of the area.

However I was only working at the computer for about fifteen or twenty minutes when the little "goat"— excuse me, "bunny"—scampered up on top of the carpets out of nowhere, so it seemed, and jumped onto the table. The keyboard seemed to be the unit that intrigued him most, as once before with the typewriter. After he thoroughly checked out the computer and the accessories, I picked him up and put him on the floor. However, sometimes if he has a keen interest in something he can be quite persistent and will not be denied but will promptly go back. I then decide it's time to call it quits and cover the equipment with a heavy cloth and find other things to do. Therefore, I was glad when he decided to look for new things to investigate, for now I had the job of removing Button's hairs from the computer and its units. It seems the electrostatic charges present on the components attract any loose hairs from his body. Even though he periodically gets a grooming with a comb and brush, especially during the times he is shedding, there is always enough left to be attracted to the computer and the accessories.

Button hadn't chewed on anything except food for a long time—at least I saw no evidence around that he had. However, one evening after having changed to a new pair of bedroom slippers, I turned to reading the paper. After a few minutes I felt a tugging on the one slipper. As I glanced down at my foot, there was Button nipping away at the raised seam of the footwear. I moved that foot away from him, so he went to work on the other one. In turn I moved that one away from him. He then decided to take a nap nearby. As I finished reading the paper I looked for Button and looked down at my slippers, and was I surprised and amazed how much he had chewed. I was so engrossed in reading that I did not realize he was working at the footwear so lightly I did not feel any tugging. Needless to say, as the days went by keeping Button at a distance when I had those slippers on wasn't easy, as he would sneak a bite now and then. And soon I was ready for a new pair. Strangely enough, Button did not bother my street shoes. They must have a different taste and of course texture to the material as well.

This brings to mind how mischievous Button can be. One day I was outside cleaning the lawn mower in the driveway near the garage entrance after cutting the grass. Button was close by. Of course I had him out near me only when I could keep an eye on him. At first he was curious as to what I was doing. The lawn mower was not new to him, as he had seen it often, as he romped around it when he was amusing himself in the workshop. Since it did not interest him, he decided to wander into the garage. As I was busy removing clusters of grass from underneath the mower, I did not see him when he came out. But as I looked up I saw that Button had hopped over to two potted flowers a few feet away from where I was working. As he was only smelling the plants, I went back to work. However, when I looked up again a short time later, Button had one of the flowerpots turned over with the plant completely out of the pot and was looking at what he had done. Since it was too late to stop him, I quickly picked up the camera, which was nearby, and took a couple

"That was fun, but what is the lady going to say about this?"

of pictures. But a few seconds later another picture presented itself, with Button placing his paws up to his chin, as if to say, "Oh! Oh! What is the lady going to say about this?" (I always referred to my sister Terry as "the lady" when speaking to Button about her.)

I should have known he was capable of doing that, as several times in the past he had dug up various plants in Terry's flower garden, until I placed a small wire fence around the area. Of course when she discovered this she would chide him and call him a naughty bunny.

The plant wasn't damaged, however, so I repotted it and reassured Button that everything was all right by petting him and scratching his nose and ears.

One day as I was reading, Button was completely stretched out alongside his food and water dishes, with his head close to the one partially filled with pellets—not a care in the world, it seemed. I think what was going through his mind was, *While I am completely relaxed, I might as well have a snack*, for he raised his head a little and reached for a pellet here and there. But as those within reach were soon all gone, I wondered what he was going to do. Of course I stopped reading, as this pending decision was becoming interesting. For a few moments he stopped reaching and then laid his head down between his paws. But not for long—for the food got the upper hand. Up jumped Button and thus he proceeded to munch at the pellets with relish, then to his other dishes, which contained the rolled oats and wheat bread.

Besides the above mentioned food, he was also given some clover and a bit of parsley, when available, at least once a day. This was pretty much Button's daily fare as he was getting older. Every so often I would give him a yogurt treat in solid form. He really loves that and needs no second invitation when I show him the sweet and drop it in his dish.

Of course Button does not eat everything at one time, as a cat or dog would. He eats intermittently, as rabbits normally do, and will go back to his dishes to partake of the contents from time to time. I've seen Button, comfortably asleep, suddenly awaken, go to his food, have a short snack and a drink of water, and back again to the same place for more napping.

I make sure that the pellets and water are always available. In fact, he has two water containers in the basement and one in the kitchen. As for the goodies, he gets those at certain times of the day and late evening. Sometimes when Button is in the kitchen and his dish of rolled oats or bread is empty and he has a desire for that fare, he will stand by that dish and bang it with his paw to attract attention to the fact that it is empty. Needless to say, he gets a refill quite promptly, to his satisfaction. For how could anyone ignore those big beautiful eyes looking right up at him?

As a rule, I make sure Button has his food before we sit down to eat. On one occasion, though, he was down in the basement as we were eating. He can come upstairs very quietly. I felt a banging on my leg and knew Button had come up. I looked down and saw that his favorite food dish under the table was empty. Since I was almost through eating, I said, "Okay, little boy, soon as I finish I'll give you yours." The next thing I knew he was on my lap—as much as to say, "I'll eat with you if you don't feed me now."

Button is very affectionate and playful, and when in that active mood he will follow us around the house and to the basement. He especially likes to romp around when I am doing some work there or my sister is doing the laundry. Sometimes he takes a notion to

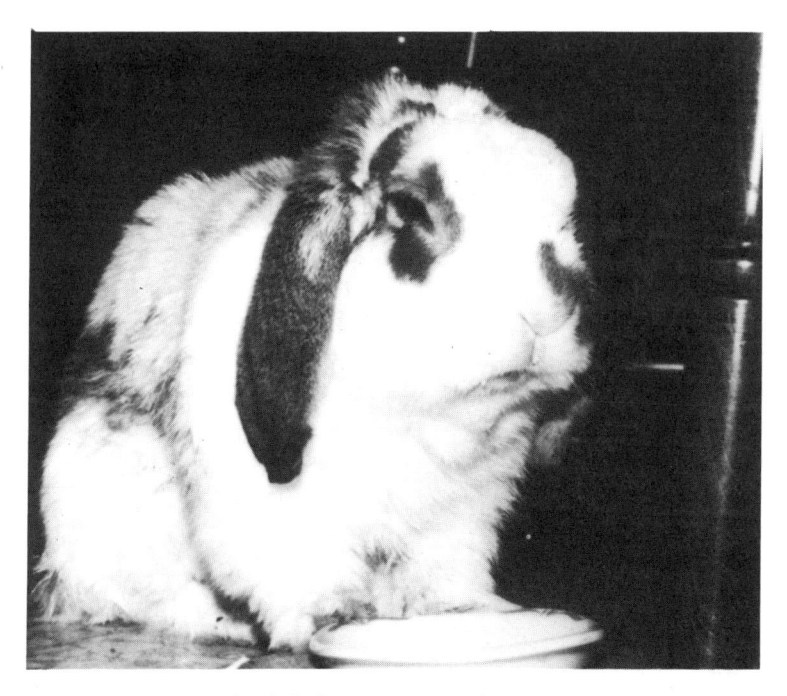

"My food dish is empty and I'm hungry."

push around a Styrofoam block about a foot square and four inches high or a small cardboard box. When he gets tired of that he will push around a metal rattle. I think the noise it makes intrigues him. Other times when he is in the basement alone amusing himself, we can hear the sound of that toy upstairs.

A favorite activity of Button is putting his front paws on top of the Styrofoam block and sort of chewing at them. Cats and dogs do the same thing. When I asked a veterinarian about this he said he wasn't sure but thought it could be due to itching between the toes.

Occasionally Button will amuse himself by scratching at a newspaper until it is well shredded or a filled grocery bag. He rarely misses an opportunity to go for the plastic trash bag after I fill it up and tie it. When I am busy elsewhere, he will jump on top of it or scratch at it near the bottom, making several holes. It is then I have to take it away, or the trash would soon be falling out.

One of Button's favorite pastimes, when he is in a playful mood, which is quite often, is to run circles around me as I try to ruffle his fur on his back as he dashes by. Sometimes he runs under a chair or table and then around me to complete the circle as I try to reach out to him. He really hops, but he goes so fast it appears more like running. Needless to say I enjoy the little game of "catch me if you can" also.

As Button got older, his field of pleasures and amusements increased. Most people buy toys for their pets to play with, and we are no exception—Button has his assortment of playthings, too, provided by myself, my sisters, and our nieces. Besides a stuffed puppy and teddy bear he also has several action toys. Among them are a kitten and a little doggie that barks, sits up, and walks, which my sister Ethell from nearby Cleveland, Ohio, bought for him. Sometimes when visiting here she will play with Button, placing a small hat on his head as he romps with the toy as if it were alive.

This brings to mind a time when Ethell was trying on different hats on his head, because he looks so cute with one placed at a rakish position. After a few minutes Button just wasn't in the mood to try on hats anymore, but as Ethell persisted, he took a nip at her hand and banged away with his paws at her. Of course he could have hopped to another area but instead stood his ground and took a defensive stance. This all happened around a small TV stand, and as she laughingly

"This is fun—push a key and a letter appears."

Button tries his hand (pardon me) his paw at pushing the wagon.

Button enjoying his periodic grooming by Lillian—or is he?

Button trying to tell Terry how much he loves his wagon.

Terry takes Button for a ride on the driveway.

"Chippy" really loves his watermelon.

Nina and her trophies, with the proud Grand Champion Oreo.

Smurfette and her five-month-old daughter Smurfin'.

"I may look cute, but I don't feel cute."

backed away and around the stand, Button went in pursuit. Ethell's husband, Lou, and I just laughed at the antics. It was really funny. The little "fella" is not one to hold a grudge for long, and in no time he and Ethell were buddies again, as she petted and scratched him around the ears—only no more hats.

I sort of drifted away from commenting on Button's collection of toys, didn't I? One that he seems to have a good deal of fun with is a hopping, standing bunny about half the size of Button, which my niece Lillian from Long Island sent to him. One can only laugh while watching as the toy is in motion. Button will nudge it with his head on one side or the other or push at it from the front. I am not sure what Button has in mind, as he will also beat the mechanical bunny with his paws as if to get him to stand still, so they can communicate, I presume. Yet other times when the toy is just sitting there motionless in a corner by the side of an easy chair Button will hop over to it, nudging it first one way and then another and no doubt wondering why it is not responding.

However, I believe Button's favorite toy is the stuffed brown and white "do nothing" doggie. Perhaps it reminds him of Penny, our lovable Pekingese-spaniel pet for eighteen years. They were great pals and quite fond of each other for the year and a half they had together. It was not unusual to see Button hop straight to it when he came into the living room, affectionately licking the ears and sometimes taking a nap alongside his favorite.

When Lillian is visiting here with her husband, Douglas, to spend some time with her mother, Button can be sure of more than the usual attention. Since they love animals and have a small dachshund named

Mousie and a cat called Callie, it did not surprise me to see Button getting a regular grooming. Needless to say, he loves the combing and brushing of his fur.

My sister told me how attached Mousie becomes to her when she visits her daughter and family, following her around. She also mentioned how Mousie likes to be covered with a small special blanket when taking a nap. It's not unusual to see Mousie pulling the blanket over herself up to the neck.

Besides the cat and dog there were also at one time three riding horses. One from that group, called Coverall, was a real family pet. He was an excellent jumper, and Terry's granddaughter Joanne frequently rode him at horse shows, winning many ribbons. I saw and petted him myself while wishfully thinking I would like to have a horse like that.

Coverall was quite intelligent. Every time someone came out of the house he would come running alongside the corral fence as close as he could to that person with his familiar neigh. Of course he was looking forward to being petted and possibly receiving a treat of some kind. Coverall was a bit of a rascal, too. On a number of occasions he managed to unlatch the doors to the stalls of the other horses, letting them out. The latches were then changed to a more complicated type. However, he figured that one out, too, and set his pals free again. It was therefore necessary to use a padlock.

Lillian and Doug relate stories about the animals on Long Island. Since they live around a wooded area, there seems to be an abundance of raccoons and foxes, but there are no rabbits in the neighborhood, as the fox is a known predator of cottontails. As to the raccoons, one would not think that goldfish had anything to fear from them, yet they manage to scoop them out of a pond nearby the house. The only alternative was to place a wire screen over the basin. The raccoon can also be quite bold. As Callie, the cat, likes to eat and sleep in the attached garage, a small swinging door leading to the outside was installed for her. Thus she can come and go at will. However, the raccoons also discovered the means of getting into the garage and eating up all of Callie's food. Therefore it was necessary to latch the small door at night after she was in.

This brings me back to Button. As a day would be coming to a close and the sun soon to set, I would put out some food for the outdoor mammals and birds. Next came taking down the barrier in front of the garage so the door could be closed. First, however, Button had to be coaxed into the workshop or breezeway. Sometimes he was quite accommodating and would readily come when called. But on certain occasions, when Button was in a playful mood, it wasn't that easy. He would dart from under one car to the other as I would get close to him. Sometimes I stood between the vehicles and tried to catch him as he zoomed by me. He was just too smart for me. I would then remove the barricade, and in no time he came out on the driveway, from where I would shoo him into the breezeway.

One day while I was sweeping the basement, Button was sitting on a small carpet I wanted to pick up. After I moved him to one side, he would promptly come right back to the same spot. So I decided to take up one end of it and drag it to the end of the room, thinking he would hop off. No way—Button never budged. In fact, he loved the ride so much, I dragged the carpet with him on it all over the basement floor. Right then an idea occurred to me—if he loved to ride so much, why not a small wagon of his own?

After visiting a number of stores that carried toys, I came to the conclusion that a suitable cart not too large or too small for Button would be difficult to find. I then decided to make one. When it was finished I placed it on the floor. Button was at one end of the basement amusing himself, and knowing how curious he can be, I just waited until he spotted it. It did not take long before he hopped over to investigate what it was and promptly jumped into the wagon. Of course I then proceeded to ride him around. It was obvious he really enjoyed it. Either my sister or I would occasionally take him for a ride indoors or outdoors on the driveway.

"I feel like taking a ride. Anyone for pulling my wagon?"

There were times when I was busy doing some chore at the entrance to the garage and I would take Button out with me and place his cart nearby, so he could play around with it if he so desired. Sure enough, he would hop upon it from one side, off again, then try the other side. Or he just put his front two paws upon it as if to push it. I think what was going through his mind was, *How do you make this thing go?* It was so amusing to watch him.

When Button is in the garage, sometimes he is in that lazy mood when he will just lie there behind the barrier, peering through the wire watching the variety of birds feeding or bathing just a few feet away. On occasion one of the wild bunnies will appear and eat with our feathered friends. They don't seem to mind at all. Now and then a gray or red squirrel will also show up looking for nuts, as I usually leave some around for them.

Speaking about squirrels, there are a number of them in the area of ours and our adjoining neighbors' backyards. It is a pleasure to watch the bushy-tailed creatures, especially when two of them get together. Much like kittens, they will roll around and wrestle. However, they can be destructive, too, as one neighbor can attest to what they can do. Jim told me how the squirrels bury their nuts that they acquire in the potted flowers that his wife Suzue has at various places on the front porch. Suzue wasn't exactly pleased with the little rascals digging up her plants, not only when they buried the nuts, but also when they went about retrieving them. As she loves flowers and animals, too, it has been a problem as what to do, since she has quite a few potted plants on the porch. She said, "I just keep my fingers crossed—so to speak—and hope they will hide their nuts in the grass or around outdoor plants," which they often do. Jim said he was working on an idea of using a small wire screen covering the soil in the pot.

My sister has also noticed a flower here and there that was uprooted in her flower bed.

We have a Carpathian walnut tree under which the birds feed and bathe. However, it seldom produces nuts, due, I believe, to climatic conditions. But I noticed the squirrels favor the tree. From time to time they will chew off a tiny branch, which falls to the ground. I concluded there must be some taste of walnuts in the foliage. The nuts do look and taste like the English walnut.

While on the topic of squirrels, I am reminded that their cute cousins the chipmunks have not been so numerous of late around our neighborhood. Only on occasion can one be seen scampering about, whereas in the past there were quite a number of them. At one time I noticed several holes in the ground on one side of the breezeway where they lived. I used to place some food for them nearby, and invariably it was gone the next day. They also found their way inside the breezeway. At one time during early spring I had some young tomato plants growing in a box, awaiting transplanting to the garden. One morning the plants were gone, roots and all. I assumed the chipmunks had quite a feast.

I attribute the scarcity of the lovable "chippies" in this area now due to the red squirrels, as they do not get along too well. It has been only recently that the red species became more numerous. There always were gray squirrels around, however.

This also reminds me of the stories a friend and

ex-coworker has been telling me about chipmunks on a small island in Maine. Dick and I used to work together in electronic research. When he retired, he and his wife, Laura, acquired this small island. They both love animals and the outdoors. Although their permanent residence is in Pennsylvania, they spend the winters in Florida and the warmest part of the summers in Maine. We have always kept in touch, and from time to time Laura and Dick write and send pictures of some of the antics of the chipmunks living there. It did not take long for them to be accepted by those adorable creatures, as shown by some of the photos. They would also readily accept treats and scamper up their clothing to eat out of the hands. It was obvious they sensed no harm was intended for them.

The lifespan of a chipmunk can reach six or seven years and longer. Dick also mentioned that the one predator they have to look out for is the hawk. Since Dick and Laura have been going to Maine for a number of years, they became familiar with the "chippies' " habits and where some of them lived. A number of them made their homes close to the cabin. After a time they not only were able to recognize certain ones, but they gave them names to which they responded. As Button had a favorite delicacy—the banana—the "chippies" had theirs, the watermelon and its seeds. They just loved it.

I am sure Dick and Laura are very much missed when they are away, and conversely their thoughts must frequently go back to the little island and their small friends, when they are in Pennsylvania or Florida.

There are times when Button will pick up a little

smudge on his nice white and brown fur here and there, romping around the garage, workshop, and a section of the breezeway where garden tools and supplies are kept. Although these areas are kept quite clean and well swept, he manages to brush up against some piece of equipment that has lubricant on it. I then lightly sponge him off and dry his fur with a towel.

However, on rare occasions he really got himself dirty by digging in damp black soil around the flower beds. This then called for a shampoo bath, as I was more concerned with the chemicals in the fertilizer that was mixed with the ground, which could give Button reactions. I know he doesn't especially care to be soaked to the skin but resigns himself to being washed. I have learned from a veterinarian who is an expert on rabbits that it is all right to bathe them, but they should be well dried afterward. This I proceeded to do, first with towels and then with a hair dryer. The whole procedure takes only a few minutes, as I made sure I had everything ready. I am sure Button felt better afterward.

My nephew who is a retired air force colonel and now working and living with his family near Denver, Colorado, is well acquainted with a family whose daughter raises French-Lop show rabbits. Nina has won many trophies with her bunnies—state as well as at fairs. But more recently she won the trophy that is the dream of all those who raise show animals—the National Trophy. As for myself, if I won any kind of award in a highly competitive contest I would feel a great deal of personal satisfaction, as I am sure most people would. But to win the "Big One" is something else again. However, it was a repeat for Nina, for she not only won for 1990~91, but also for 1989~90 as well.

Button is probably thinking, *I did not need that bath.*

Since my nephew Bill is quite the amateur photographer, I asked him to take a picture of Nina, her trophies, and some of her proud champions the next time he and his wife, Joyce, visited Nina and her family. One of the lovable winners is named Oreo, and then there are Smurfette and her daughter Smurfin'.

Since I have never entered an animal in a show, I wasn't too familar with the procedures involved. There are several classes in which the rabbits compete. I knew judging was based on a number of attributes of the entries. With rabbits it is the condition of the fur, color, weight, alertness, etc. After the points are tallied, a first place winner in then chosen. As Nina explained to me, this is considered a leg.

To be a Grand Champion a rabbit must win three legs. Oreo and Smurfette are such winners. In fact, they have won several times over to qualify as Grand Champions. Smurfin', who is only five months old, has already won one leg.

Button has never participated in a contest, but I am sure if he were in one for intelligence, activity, and companionship he would come away with top honors. To me he is a champion in his own right. I believe pet owners everywhere probably share that feeling about their pets.

Nina puts in many hours taking care of her bunnies and the rabbitry, housed in an attached garage. It is more like a dollhouse and beautifully done inside. She decided if she was going to raise show rabbits, she was going to do it right. Therefore, she not only concentrated on the physical aspect of the interior of the rabbitry, but also the care, feeding, and health of the bunnies. This entailed lots of reading, research, and attending forums on the well-being of rabbits. Her mother and father both help Nina in various ways. Her father applies techniques used in his own business in keeping the rabbitry spotless.

Since domestic rabbits are delicate creatures when

"That wasn't a very interesting program."

it comes to their digestive systems, it is important that they have proper food to eat and preventive medication periodically. It is also important that they have the right treatment when they do develop some ailment. Most veterinarians will use or recommend one that is more suitable for cats and dogs. Of course there are veterinarians who specialize in certain small animals, but one is not always readily available when needed.

When Button was ailing my nephew Bill put me in touch with Nina and she promptly sent me some special medication. She is a very understanding and caring person. I have talked to her on the phone on numerous occasions and have learned a good deal from her experience on the care and feeding of rabbits.

An affectionate pet is really a joy to have around. Animals seem to understand so much. I'm thinking back to not too long ago, when I was confined to a wheelchair for several weeks because of an accident. I know Button must have wondered why I wasn't up and about with him as before, for we were two active individuals. He seemed to accept the fact that I could not get around as in the past, for he spent more time with me upstairs in the living room and kitchen than down in the basement. If he wasn't up on my lap to be petted or brushed and combed, he was on the coffee table near me when I was sitting on the couch. If I decided to take a nap there, I could be sure Button would eventually jump over alongside me.

Most people spoil their pets, and I am no exception. I know Button involves extra work sometimes, such as cleaning up after he overturns his water or food dish, shreds a newspaper, or rumples a carpet. However, I feel a lot like the lady I read about not so long ago. She had a turkey for a pet that had the run of the house pretty much as would a cat or dog—or bunny! Friends noticed this gobbler pulled things out of place here and there and asked if she wasn't tired of putting things back. She replied, "No way. If it were not for my pet, I would not get half the exercise I need." Without going into details, I believe the lady said it all.

In conclusion, I would like to add that different people like different pets. Sometimes it depends on the

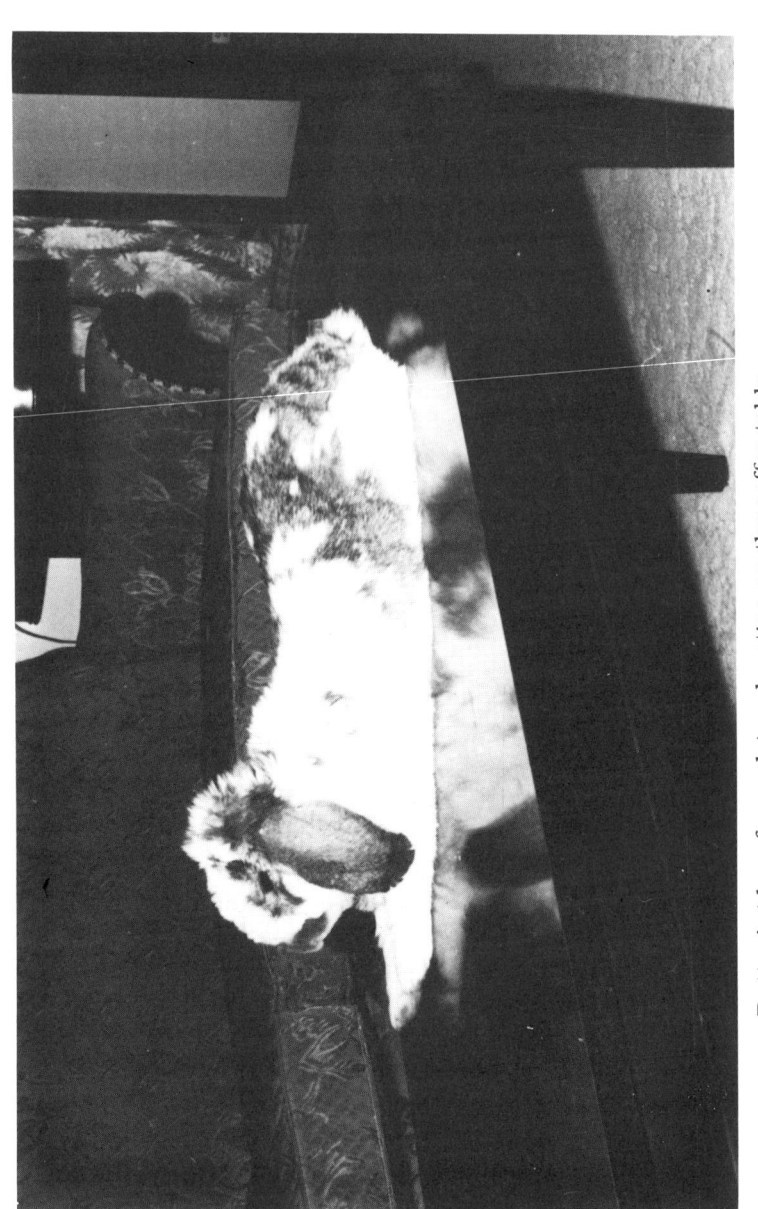

Button's idea of complete relaxation on the coffee table.

environment and their ability to take care of them. Also, there are those who relate more to one species of pets than another, deriving from the pet the pleasure of companionship they have not found in the company of other people.